Jan

Navigating
THE RIVER OF TIME

Enjoy the story!

Navigating
THE RIVER OF TIME
THE ADVENTURES OF JOAQUIN & OLIVIER

GILBERT LE GRAS

Order this book online at www.trafford.com
or email orders@trafford.com

Most Trafford titles are also available at major online book retailers.

© Copyright 2015 Gilbert Le Gras.

All rights reserved. No part of this publication may be reproduced, stored in a retrieval system, or transmitted, in any form or by any means, electronic, mechanical, photocopying, recording, or otherwise, without the written prior permission of the author.

Print information available on the last page.

ISBN: 978-1-4907-6170-1 (sc)
ISBN: 978-1-4907-6171-8 (hc)
ISBN: 978-1-4907-6169-5 (e)

Library of Congress Control Number: 2015910412

Because of the dynamic nature of the Internet, any web addresses or links contained in this book may have changed since publication and may no longer be valid. The views expressed in this work are solely those of the author and do not necessarily reflect the views of the publisher, and the publisher hereby disclaims any responsibility for them.

Any people depicted in stock imagery provided by Thinkstock are models, and such images are being used for illustrative purposes only.
Certain stock imagery © Thinkstock.

Trafford rev. 06/29/2015

 www.trafford.com

North America & international
toll-free: 1 888 232 4444 (USA & Canada)
fax: 812 355 4082

This work of fictionalized genealogy is meant to convey my values and culture to my sons, Olivier and Joaquín. It is dedicated to my parents, André Le Gras and Yolande Le Gras (née Gamache), who taught me the importance of faith, family, and integrity. It is also meant to show history through a personal lens to my sons Olivier and Joaquín and their friends about their family roots over 270 years.

'Blessed are the peacemakers, for they will be called the children of God.'

Matthew 5:9

Chapter 1

I remember crouching down and staring ahead when I felt a darkness twist tightly around me and objects distorting into different shapes and sizes. Then the light dimmed and the muscles throughout my body flexed to what felt like their physical limits before I sensed something like waking up – except I found myself in a new place and time.

"Ga aan! De slag met!" someone was yelling at me through what seemed like a tunnel. Crouched down on uneven ground, my head and limbs felt weighed down and stiff. My skin was sweaty and sticky. Through heavy eyelids, I could make out that whoever was yelling at me was about to bring down a crashing blow over my head. Despite the nauseating pit in my stomach and dizziness in my head, I gathered what strength I had and raised my arm to break the blow.

I was astonished to see my left arm was sheathed in a metal skin, just before it deflected my attacker's sword away from my buzzing skull. The blade dragged along my forearm to the elbow with a high screech piercing my eardrums just as I was rising up and losing my balance. The fall opened my attacker's arms wide in either direction before I fell face forward – throwing my entire body's weight into an unintended head butt directly into the bull's-eye of a red shield emblazoned on his tunic.

"Only you would use your whole body as a battering ram," laughed another man who dismounted his horse and extended his hand to me while his footman pinned my attacker down. "Would you like to give this Dutchman a close shave?" he asked as he pulled a single-handed grip sword from the pool of muddy water next to where I'd be crouching.

"No," I croaked back in a hoarse voice parched from my recovery from unconsciousness.

"Fine, I'll claim this kill," he replied.

"I don't have much use for a left-handed singlestick," he said as he turned his pale blue eyes in my direction. "It's only Tuesday and this is our third assault on the Dutch line, so see to it that your next duel isn't with another southpaw like you. Being left-handed might not be so much of an advantage then."

Not far from me was another cavalryman kneeling down, closer to the river bank, retching yellow bile and breathing hard. I thought to myself that he looked like I was feeling. But on a closer look, and to my surprise, I recognized his face.

It was my brother.

Infantry bearing the same azure colours as my brother and my rescuer on their tunics advanced past us. Many were singing *La Marche Henri IV* while others were laughing and jostling each other, leaving me with the distinct impression that my experience of this conflict was the exception rather than the rule.

> "Vive Henri quatre
> Vive ce Roi vaillant
> Ce diable à quatre
> À le triple talent!"

Some of the infantry were bearing banners and pennants of the Kingdom of France's *Royal Standard* – a white field adorned with 39 gilded Fleurs de Lys overlaid with the *France Moderne* azure shield containing three more of the golden, stylized lilies – a simplified version of the *France Ancienne* coat of arms that seemed to now be the ubiquitous symbol decorating the mass of troops advancing ahead of us.

I called out to Olivier over the loud, confusing mixture of noises made by more than 100,000 French soldiers marching on what appeared to be an inferior number of Dutch, British and Hanoverian cavalry and infantry.

"Are you alright?"

"I think so…I'm not sure what happened just now," Olivier answered, shaking his head and spitting bile to the ground. "Where are we?"

"You boys are a long way off from the Forest of Orient," my rescuer called out as he mounted his chestnut coloured Arabian mare, pointing to the coat of arms emblazoned on my saddle pad. "Don't you remember? It's the Marshal General of France, Maurice de Saxe, who enlisted you in Louis XV's army to come to fight in the Austrian Netherlands."

"Now get to your horses before you end up having to swim to Rocoux," he said, nodding to a gray filly and a black gelding grazing about a dozen metres away as he fitted his blue tricorne hat back on his head, saluted us and rode in the direction of the advancing column of infantrymen and reconstituting cavalry formation.

"It could be worse," he added. "You could have been with my brother JeanMaurice trying to retake Louisbourg from the British over in New France. Thank God he's sailing back home on *Le Mars* now."

Olivier clasped me with each hand on my shoulders and helped me steady myself on my feet.

"Joaquín, where are we and what are we doing here?"

I shook my head, which Olivier took to mean I didn't know. In this manner of speaking it could have been true. But, really, I was trying to find the words to explain to myself as much as to him that it appeared that somehow we had been catapulted back nearly three centuries in time.

We would soon piece together, from questions we put to each of our footmen while feigning we'd sustained concussions in the mêlée, that we'd landed on the banks of the oldest river in the world which was currently serving as the front line in what would soon no longer be separating the Holy Roman Empire from the Kingdom of France.

It was Tuesday, October 11, 1746, and we were about to ford the Meuse River on horseback to play our part in securing a decisive French victory in the War of the Austrian Succession.

Chapter 2

As a child, I remember watching snails edge along the hot stone pavement at my grandparents' summer cottage and I wondered if time moved at a different pace for them than it did for us. My father's answer puzzled me then, but I told myself it would become clearer as I grew older. Little did I realize that I would need time to turn back for its fluid nature to truly reveal itself.

"You know, time is a puzzle that's stumped physicists as much as philosophers and anthropologists," my father was telling me one evening as he wound up his stainless steel 1979 Omega Speedmaster Moonwatch Professional before putting me to bed.

I used to like weighing the exotic looking wristwatch in the palm of my hand. It was heavy and it wasn't the matching stainless steel bracelet that accounted for much of the weight of this 14-mm thick waterproof time piece. It was the complex array of gears and wheels and springs hidden behind the watch's mesmerizing black dial and glow-in-the-dark tritium hour markers. In the dark, it gave the illusion of a black hole sucking in errant rays of light as I'd watch my father reach for my shoulder before he'd kiss me good night.

Even though most people relied on their smart phones or digital watches, there was always something that drew me to Dad's old-school time piece and its historical ties to the early years of humanity's exploration of space.

One day, while I was weighing it in my hands, I thought of flipping it over to see if I could open it to study its entrails. I noticed the inscription on the back: "Flight qualified by NASA for all manned space missions – The first watch worn on the Moon." At the centre of this inscription was a graven image of a sea dragon with "Speedmaster" crowning its head and the uppercase version of the last letter of the Classical Greek alphabet – Omega, the symbol of the end of time – beneath it.

I remembered all this because while we forded the Meuse River, I could see the reflection of my family's coat of arms on my saddle pad off the surface of the water. It was an azure shield with a silver bend drawn from the top left-hand corner to the bottom right-hand edge that separated two dragons' heads on either side.

This is what reminded me of my father's curious answer to my question:

"I think of time as a stream of water. It flows forward into an unknown direction from a distant and imperceptible source," he explained. "And it's a reflection of our perceptions too. When you exchange messages with your grandmother on the Pacific Coast over the Internet, you're separate by several time zones but you are sharing the same moment in time – a bit like two pieces of wood floating roughly in parallel with each other on a river stream. Or when I go Scuba diving in an underground river that has sea water under the soft water, it's as if there's a liquid mirror separating them and reflecting a distorted image of myself. In many ways, time is an illusion."

I wondered about this explanation as my gaze wandered from the reflection of my coat of arms to the undulating reflection of my gelding, gently gliding through the water while I remained kneeling on his back.

I looked further and saw pools of smooth and flat river water.

My father had taught me that you can read water like you can read a book. He had been Scuba diving for decades so he would often jump into the ocean first to scout the conditions. He told me that it was always best to avoid diving into a patch of flat and smooth water because it was a telltale sign of turbulence, a place where two or more currents collided causing unpredictable switches in the ebb and flow of those bodies of water.

Maybe this explained what appeared to be our leap through space-time – had Olivier and I stumbled onto a segment of the flow of time that ran against the grain of space? If that were the case, and this was all part of a turbulent stream, then what might we expect next?

I was jolted out of my reverie when my gelding's front hooves struck the rising river bed, prompting me to lower my legs to its side and settle back into my saddle. Instinctively, I reached for my flintlock musket while holding onto the reigns with my right hand.

"I have an idea that might explain how we got here," I yelled out to Olivier.

"I'm dying to find out, but it will have to wait," he called back, reaching for his firearm while his filly followed closely behind me as they emerged from the murky depths of this 380-million-year-old river.

Having crossed this natural barrier seemed to deliver a blow to the opposing camp's morale and, from the vantage point of standing up in my stirrups and judging from the dwindling number of standards that remained immobile; it looked as though a small number of British cavalry were reinforcing a rear-guard line of British, Hanoverian and Dutch infantry.

Although dusk was upon us, the sky brightened with streaks of bright red flames hurtling toward the line of troops awaiting us just off the muddy banks of the river and in front of the fortifications of Liège and its castle further behind them, atop a steep hill. The immediate effect of this bombardment was to disperse much of their line of defence before we reached their position.

"This will be a glorious day for our King," declared my footman, who had not yet learned to swim and made the crossing by clinging to one of my stirrups.

"I'd rather see the late Cardinal Fleury get the credit than that perpetual adolescent," said Olivier's footman.

"Mind your loyalties," interjected my rescuer, who had crossed the river alongside us. "The King has no more need of a first minister since the good Cardinal passed away more than three years ago. You dishonour the house of Le Gras de St-Germain with such revolutionary talk."

It was Olivier's turn to wade into political waters, and as usual, his negotiating skills defused the situation.

"We are grateful for your assistance on the other shore," he replied. "But my footman Louis-Sébastien is no doubt reflecting my high regard for the Cardinal's excellent administrative skills. It is, after all, thanks to him that France has the most modern and extensive road system in all of Europe, making the journey here much easier for all of us. Not to mention the best standing army of our time."

Our companion pulled a face, but recognizing that he had stepped out of his boundaries in rebuking one of our footmen, he seized the out Olivier offered him to maintain his image before his own servant.

"True. The King chose well to delegate his authorities to such a capable man while he was still becoming familiar with the affairs of state. We mourn his loss to this day. And the King is growing into the job of administrator in addition to his responsibilities as regent," he concluded, before spurring his mare in her hindquarters to pursue the retreating enemy infantry.

The four of us darted looks at one another and then to our immediate surroundings before anyone broke the silence. I was about to speak up when Olivier's footman, Louis-Sébastien Mercier, took the initiative.

"I'm sorry, my lord, I did not realize anyone was close enough to us to overhear what we were discussing," he said.

Between Olivier's clearly sharper recollection of history and Louis-Sébastien's statement, we both surmised that being senior public administrators thanks to our recent inclusion in the nobility of Troyes, some 300 kilometres to the south, meant that we probably shared his political views. But common sense and a quick assessment of the mood of the times led all of us to conclude that we should keep those views privately among us.

"While I don't dispute what you say, I would not want our private views to be exposed publicly on a breaking wheel," Olivier replied, in reference to the medieval torture device still in use in the mid-18th century for capital punishment. "Why don't you keep those ideas in the fantasy stories you're so fond of writing in your spare time?"

It always amazed me how Olivier could remember details like the breaking wheel, which in these circumstances suddenly felt a lot less trivial to me. It must be from playing video games like Assassin's Creed for so many hours. Some of the period's historical details were bound to stick, I told myself. If only our current predicament were nothing more than the latest generation in computer gaming, I wouldn't be so preoccupied about what might be coming next. Unfortunately, it was beginning to dawn on me that my better recollection of our family's history might not serve as much of a guide.

Chapter 3

I swallowed hard. Now that I'd explained my hunch to Olivier that space-time turbulence landed us here, it was time to break the worse news.

"Look, I remember our family history book saying that Pierre-Édouard Le Gras married the noble lady Delle Marie-Edmée Baillot in January 1748 in Troyes, and *that's* when our family was granted the noble title 'de St-Germain'. That's 14 months from now. So something's slightly off which means I can't predict what's next," I explained to my elder brother while we were alone in our field tent.

Now it was Olivier's turn to try his hand at speculating on our predicament.

"Ok, let's take a step back. So, we have been living in the regular streamline of space and time until something or someone knocked both of us into a turbulent patch, right?"

I nodded my agreement in the glow of the lamp dangling overhead. But before I could say anything more, a fist clutching a dagger pulled back the flap of our tent, exposing the face of my rescuer just before he blew out the candle in our lamp.

"That's quite the imagination you two have there," our erstwhile compatriot whispered into our ears as he lay down between each of our heads, and pressed the cold sharp edges of the knives he clutched in both of his hands against the skin of each of our necks.

"We like to tell each other stories before going to sleep," Olivier replied in a hushed voice.

"If it were your footman telling me this, I would believe it," he snarled back. "In fact, I know your stories are going to inspire a very successful book he will write in 25 years from now called 'The Year 2440: A Dream If Ever There Was One'."

"Sure, and I'm going to be the next King of France," I snapped back at him.

"Not if you value your life," he chuckled. "I'm from the future too, so there's no need for me to tell you what will happen to him."

He had a point, as did the sharp edge of his blade pressed against my jugular. Everyone from the 19th century onward knew the abrupt fate of another Austrian monarch, Marie-Antoinette, and the next King of France in about 50 years at the losing end of the blade on a guillotine outside Paris' infamous, vermin-infested Bastille prison.

"So, what is it with you? You save my life at dusk so you can take it at dawn," I whispered, reckoning the game was up for Olivier and me.

"Shut up and listen, or I might just grant you your wish," he replied, lifting the blades from our throats.

Chapter 4

"Just over three weeks ago there was a total solar eclipse in the Southern Hemisphere which means the Moon blocks out the Sun from our view, but it also means the Earth blocks out some of its rays as well," the stranger explained. "This blots out just enough light from our Sun that fewer rays of light are absorbed by a black hole in the Cygnus constellation which is only a quarter of the way from here to the centre of our galaxy. In other words: uncomfortably close.

"Black holes are massive objects whose gravity is so powerful even light can't escape it. It's possible that a bit less light from our Sun caused some turbulence in space-time which landed you here," he added.

In a way, it made sense. But it was a chilling conclusion that we'd fallen into a tear in the fabric of space-time. It also implied that fragments of streamlined space-time had been slightly disjointed and the consequences of that were beyond all our imaginations. And finally, the only way to sustain a turbulent flow requires a persistent source of energy driving it, otherwise it dissipates quickly.

What he hadn't said, but seemed clearly obvious now, was that this phenomenon was fundamentally unstable so we were either going to remain stuck in the mid-18th century or get flung back and forth again a few more times, depending on the strength of the original source of the turbulence and the duration of that trigger.

I knew this same conclusion had dawned on Olivier when he whispered a dismayed whistle.

"What makes you so sure this is like turbulence in water?" Olivier asked, hopefully.

"Your symptoms seemed to be a lot like severe motion sickness," he answered. "You told your footmen that everything went dark and that you both felt like you were spinning into a whirlpool. Your eyes couldn't see any change but your sense of balance was completely thrown off. The brain can't reconcile those two contradictions, so it's hardwired to make your bodies react as though it was poisoned and that's why you threw up."

"O.k., but then why do I remember Joaquín being with me when everything went dark but I don't ever remember setting eyes on you before now," Olivier continued.

He let out a sigh, and scratched the nape of his neck.

"Look. The less you know about all of this the better. Trust me," he said.

"Why should either of us trust you," I answered. "We saw you kill that Dutchman, then you ambush us in our tent with daggers drawn on our throats and tell us this fantastic story after eavesdropping on us. What's to say you aren't telling us a lethal bedtime story?"

Cursing under his breath, he planted both knifes in the blanket we'd spread over the wet mud we were lying on and sat cross legged.

"Maybe this will convince you," he said. "As I overheard you say, Pierre-Édouard marries into nobility in 14 months from now. But neither of you mentioned that three years after that, Delle gives birth to Antoine-Édouard who, 35 years later, is appointed as a prison warden by King Louis XVI as well as legal advisor and presiding official in Paris.

"But that appointment won't last long because in 1789 the King will be overthrown in the French Revolution and a friend warns Antoine-Édouard that revolutionaries are coming in a night raid to the prison to kill him. He'll end up hiding in a horse-drawn cart full of manure and escaping to Belgium where your family will spend the next century before immigrating to Canada on the *S.S. Sardinian* for the following century," our mysterious fortune teller added. "Shall I continue?"

After a long pause, it was Olivier who broke the silence.

"Who are you?"

Chapter 5

He slowly started opening his mouth and the sound waves drawing out of his windpipe dropped several octaves and stretched each syllable out as dark clouds blotted out the rising morning sun over his shoulder. That's when the inside of our field tent dissolved into a kaleidoscope spiral. The bottom of my stomach gave out as I realized we were being sucked under the surface of the slipstream of space-time once again.

The next moment, all the muscles in my body ached from exhaustion as I swayed slightly, standing among rows and rows of men in uniforms. A single ray of light illuminated the space around me, reflecting off the fine particles of dust that bobbed gently up and down as they drifted through the shaft of sunlight flooding in from the vaulted ceiling high above our heads. It looked like it was snowing particles of light.

Aware of the others around me, but my vision blurred by the column of light, I tried stepping back out of the light to better see my surroundings. That's when he broke my fall. He must have been no older than 14 or 15, with just the beginning of facial hair sprouting on his upper lip. The pencil mustache broke into a broad smile as he steadied me back on my feet.

"I don't know how solid these church pews are, so you'd better not drop yourself on them," he whispered into my right ear. "I'm as tired as you are from all these days of marching and fighting in Loreto and Guadalupe. It seems like that's all we've done since we landed in Veracruz two months ago with our dear general the Count Charles de Lorencez, but we're almost at Mexico City now."

Just then, the priest motioned for us to kneel and pray, invoking the name of the Saint we were honouring this Monday, May 5, 1862 – St. Maximus of Jerusalem. From this vantage point, and with my head bowed down, I could see the Napoleon III insignia on my young companion's uniform.

"Where are we?" I asked him.

"Some place called Puebla. The rumour is the Mexican general, Zaragoza, has assembled a militia at least as large as ours on the outskirts of town," he replied. "My name is Edgar, what's yours?"

"Olivier Le Gras," I answered, extending my hand as I watched his eyes widen.

"That's my name," the teenager gasped. "I'm Edgar Jean Alexandre Le Gras de St-Germain of Bruxelles. Where are you from?"

Just then, the sound of hundreds of leather boots snapping back up to attention broke our conversation, buying me precious moments to pull my thoughts together.

"I came from further away and it took some time to get here," I said, as I rose up in tandem with my Great Great Great Grandfather, who, in a few short hours would prove himself worthy of a Napoleonic Mexican campaign medal on the battlefield despite this impending and historic defeat.

Just another reason why I don't like Mondays, I suppose.

As we streamed into the centre aisle for Communion, I searched the faces shuffling along until I caught Joaquín's eye. What neither one of us expected to see was our rescuer and tormentor from northwestern Europe a century earlier acting as Eucharistic Minister – locking his pale blue eyes on my chestnut brown eyes as I walked ahead of Joaquín in his direction.

"Body of Christ," he greeted. "Amen," I replied. Then he whispered what I yearned to know. "Are you ready to hear my answer?"

Chapter 6

Joaquín and I worked our way against the flow of the soldiers streaming out of the massive stone church up the left-hand side aisle to the Sacristy, where he had instructed us to meet him. It wasn't unusual for a few soldiers to straggle behind to confess themselves before going into battle so our commanding officer just nodded us on as he walked past.

Up the stairs, and out of eyesight and earshot of the others, we turned the corner into the Sacristy behind the Altar and there he was, a looming silhouette framed by the stained-glass window.

"I've waited almost 120 years for you to answer my question, so I'll say it again: Who are you?"

He hadn't aged in the least, so Joaquín and I assumed he must be a time traveller on the same path as us.

"Patience is a virtue," he chuckled. My father always said this to me, and it grated on my nerves as much when anyone else said it to me.

"Look, we don't know what's going on but you clearly do. If you're not going to tell us, then it's because you're not interested in helping us," I said, with steel in my voice and spittle flying off my lip as the frustration tightened the muscles in my throat.

"That's a fine bit of deductive logic, young man, but you're wrong. I am here to help you. It's just that you'll find my answer to be a bit," he paused, for emphasis or dramatic effect (and possibly both), before his voice trailed off into the final word: "Fantastical."

It was Joaquín's turn to jump into the conversation:

"Really? After everything that we've been through since we met you? Let us be the judges of that. Now tell us, who are you and what's going on?"

I could hear him sigh as he pulled the vestments over his head from his back to his front in a fluid motion, fanning dusty air into our eyes as he shrugged and stated blandly: "I'm your spirit guide."

If you asked me, the blond-haired man didn't strike me as the cherubic type, but after all we'd witnessed, I was ready to take a bit of a leap of faith. So, scrubbing out as much natural skepticism as I could from my voice, I took a step back with my left leg, opened my arms to either side and uttered the following words:

"I'll be honest with you. I wasn't expecting that for an answer, but, to be frank, I really don't know what to expect any more so I'm keeping an open mind and I'm going to ask you to explain to us what's going on here," I said in as close to an as-a-matter-of-fact voice I could muster.

I could see he was weighing my attitude from the way he shifted on his feet. He was of an average height but had a muscular build on a solid frame of a body. Most adversaries would be wise to think twice before confronting this man in any conflict. He naturally commanded respect from those he encountered. Eventually, he selected his words. Carefully, he replied:

"It's simple, but complicated at the same time," he said, studying my body language for any further clues to what I was really thinking.

"Try us," Joaquín replied, hands on both sides of his waist, his green eyes fixed on our interlocutors' pale blue ones.

"Well, as you no doubt are appreciating by now, you're not really supposed to be here, chatting with your Great Great Great Grandfather and distracting him before he heads into a potentially lethal battle that is pivotal to the history of the Americas and Europe," he stated, while pacing around the Sacristy.

"Yes, go on," I prompted.

"On a few rare occasions, these things happen, so I'm sent bouncing along the same trajectory along what we call the Eternal Present as you to adjust things so they unfold largely as they're supposed to," he continued, shifting his focus to Joaquín in the hope of discerning whether or not he was accepting this explanation.

"Some people react differently," he added, testing our willingness to listen. After a long pregnant pause, he added: "I mean two things by this. Some people skip from one place to another – like you are right now – but others just live it out one-day at a time. Either way, you all eventually ask the same question and you get the answer I just gave. The catch is some people don't take it well because how and when it all goes back to the way it was depends on them, while others see it as their chance to rewrite history and that makes it worse for a lot more people."

Just then, two foreign volunteers entered the Sacristy to call Joaquín and myself to muster with our platoon. One of them was olive-skinned and stocky, with a square jaw and deep chestnut eyes. The other had a slighter build, lighter complexion and a plump, amiable face. It was uncanny how much they looked like Joaquín's schoolmates Santiago and Dante.

Our mysterious companion saw the expressions on our faces and raised his right index finger to his pursed lips, so we held our tongues.

"We're almost done with their blessings here, you two go ahead and they'll be right behind you," he said, as he clasped one hand on each of our shoulders.

Once the dust-encrusted hinges of the wooden door shut with the grinding screech of soot and dust against rust, the three of us closed a circle into a huddle

"Did those two look familiar? That's because there are only a little more than 1 billion people in the whole world at this point in time compared with more than 7 billion in the time you come from. Those two soldiers are the Great Great Great Grandfathers of your friends," he said.

I wanted to hear more of this story of people travelling through time as though they were rocks skipping on the surface of a lake, or other people who seemed to live forever. But most of all, I was just starting to understand how knowing what was supposed to happen next could be a very empowering – and dangerous – thing.

"The battle is about to begin, so I don't have time to explain everything in much detail, but just know that I am Michael, your protector and healer," and with that last comment, he turned back into the Church as we headed for the door our comrades-in-arms had just taken.

Chapter 7

I slipped on the black limestone steps of the small town's church, falling onto a short and stout man with a muscular build and jet black hair. He shoved me into Joaquín's arms and growled: "Yanki Go Home!"

Puzzled, we looked at Santiago and Dante for an explanation.

"He knows you're not from the United States. A lot of the locals are loyal to President Benito Juarez and they think the French Army is here to not only conquer Mexico but support the South in the U.S. Civil War," Santiago said.

The Mexicans had recently settled a civil war of their own between 1858 and 1860 and Juarez was their first elected president, but not everyone had accepted the outcome of either the conflict or the election.

Murals along the colourful, narrow streets of this bedroom community on the outskirts of Puebla depicted tall, light-skinned men demanding money from shorter, darker skinned men. Although our expeditionary force had stormed Veracruz with British and Spanish troops like Dante and Santiago a few months ago, they had returned home after negotiating new terms on delayed Mexican debt payments. Edgar had enlisted as surety on our family's life savings but at 14 years of age he probably hadn't bargained on becoming a pawn in an attempt by Napoléon III to establish a Second Mexican Empire.

I guess that's why they call it infantry – literally child soldiers. Sometimes leaders sell us the idea of going to war to fight the good fight, to be peacemakers and that it's a sure path to Justice or Heaven, but they're not on the front lines and have their own selfish motives driving the agenda. War – too often it's nothing more than the ultimate form of real estate.

"You should really watch where you step Olivier, the snakes are molting and there are skins everywhere," Dante warned me. "That's what you slipped on outside the Cathedral. The locals told me that before Puebla de los Angeles was founded in 1531 it was called *Cuetlaxcoapan*. It's a native word for 'where serpents shed their skins'."

How fitting, I thought to myself, that the strongest and best equipped army of this time was about to lose its footing in the land of the shedding snakes. Sometimes the afternoon downpours would cause mud slides and flash flooding, carrying snakes down the slopes of the mountains like Pico de Orizaba, or *Citlaltépetl* which means the Mountain of the Stars.

The Mountain of the Stars rises 5-1/2 kilometres (18,500 feet) above sea level. The dormant volcano is the third highest in North America and home to wild rabbits, racoons, eagles and snakes – both the poisonous and harmless kinds. What's interesting is the harmless snakes' skins mimic the markings of venomous snakes to protect themselves from predators, like eagles.

Coral snakes, for example, and red milk snakes have bands of colour on their skin alternating with yellow, red, and black bands. This way they are easily confused as one being the other.

"Just remember this trick," Edgar told us as the march got underway. "Red against yellow will kill a fellow. That's the Coral snake. But red against black is a friend of Jacques. That's the red milk snake."

This is nature's way of giving harmless animals a strategic deception advantage over its predators. People with a keen sense of observation have adapted the strategic and tactical deception advantages they have seen in nature to how to cope with their own adversaries.

"Our platoon leader told us about both forms of deception advantages from what his father witnessed in Napoléon I's Grand Army. That's when 680,000 soldiers laid siege to Moscow in 1812," Edgar panted as we marched at a brisk pace as the afternoon rain clouds gathered overhead.

"A tactical deception advantage for shorter people, like teenagers facing a full-grown man, is to come close to his longer arms that reach past us so he has to struggle against his own body armour to turn his hands back inward on us and also himself," he continued. "A strategic deception advantage is the Russians deciding to use time to their advantage and hold out against the Grand Army of 1812 until winter arrived. More than 380,000 of Napoléon's soldiers were killed, froze or starved. The rest ate their horses and had to march west back to France."

Joaquín whistled his exclamation of shock at such heavy losses, and added:

"That puts Napoléon's comment about strategy into perspective," he said.

Seeing my puzzled look, Joaquín quoted our Emperor's Corsican uncle.

"La stratégie est l'art d'utiliser le temps et l'espace. Je suis moins intéressé par le second. On peut récupérer l'espace; le temps perdu – jamais (Strategy is the art of making use of time and space. I am less concerned about the latter than the former. Space we can recover, lost time – never)," he told us.

Just then, Michael galloped up to our advancing column and ordered us to split in two different directions, sending some troops to the Fort of Loreto and the others to the Fort of Guadalupe, but ordering Joaquín and me to stay by his side.

"Now you understand your family motto on your Coat of Arms. 'Vous perdez temps' means you lose time, but not as in you are wasting time," Michael said as we marched briskly along his trotting horse.

"As Napoléon I said: 'Il y a une espèce de voleur que les lois ne recherchent pas, et qui dérobe ce que les hommes ont de plus précieux : le temps.' (There is a certain kind of thief that the authorities do not pursue and who strip men of their most precious possession: time.)," he explained, watching the two columns of infantry march to France's next Waterloo.

Just then, storm clouds gathered overhead and my head started spinning. Just before everything went dark, I thought to myself: "Here we go; it's that time again…"

Chapter 8

(Photo courtesy of Mary Anne LeGras-Nikkel)

I remember my first thought being that Olivier was throwing up again because he always suffered motion sickness more than me – but my next thought is what snapped me out of my dream state: there was no way fireflies could fly so fast, in such large numbers and all of them in straight lines.

"Get down you two, we're ambushed," the young soldier in olive-coloured flannels yelled to us, motioning us to take cover behind the engine of his pug-nose three-ton truck.

"What's going on," I asked.

"There are pockets of Wehrmacht and Waffen-SS hiding all over these woods," the infantryman told us as the flashes of light whistled overhead. "It's as intense as it was eight months ago when we landed in Normandy. They didn't put up as much of a fight in Belgium and Holland but now that we've pushed them back into Germany's Rhineland, they're fighting for their homes."

Another burst of five high-velocity rounds whizzed overhead, the last one followed by the trailing pyrotechnic charge that burned brightly to light the path of the volley's trajectory so the marksmen could correct their aim.

He flung the passenger side door open, and stood up behind it to peer through the window.

All we could see in the moonlight was the inscription on the panel riveted to the bottom of the inside of the door: This Canadian Military Pattern truck was made with pride by the Steel Body Manufacturers for the Department of Munitions and Supply in December, 1944.

Another burst of five shots rang out; this time the last two bullets were "tracers", trailed by the bright pyrotechnic charge that traced the trajectory dangerously near our comrade in arms.

"Two tracers in a row," he told us in a hushed tone. "That usually means they're out of bullets and have to load again."

Then I heard what sounded like an even louder firecracker coming from a different angle that was followed by a blinding light just above my head. Suddenly our rescuer flew backward and yelled out a sharp cough before landing several feet back onto the frozen mud and snow.

"Are you ok," I asked.

"I don't know," he gasped. "I think I've been shot." Then he passed out.

Bullets continued to whiz over our heads from the treeline on the other side of the military convoy. Then I heard the crunching of boots against the gravel and frozen pools of water on the road the caravan of vehicles had been rolling down. Suddenly, one pair of boots stopped on the other side of our truck's open door.

"Schneller! Schneller zu lauffen," a voice belonging to the boots said, before running to the other side and throwing an empty pack of Eckstein No. 5 Cigaretten with 'im Januar 1945 gemacht' stamped on the ribbon. It was January, 1945.

Chapter 9

"Olivier," I whispered to the dark form lying next to the young Canadian soldier. "Are you o.k?"

"Yeah, but he's unconscious and I think he's bleeding – it's thicker than melting snow," Olivier whispered in reply. "I think we should hide under the truck until things settle down."

I crawled along the frozen country road's gravel and empty brass shell casings as quietly as I could until I reached the injured soldier's feet. Olivier was already raising this head with one hand and right shoulder with the other.

"Ready, set, go," he said, and we dragged him and ourselves under the axle of the pug-nose truck. The soldier groaned in pain and came to his senses long enough to whisper a few words into Olivier's ear.

I could tell from his body language that whatever he said was not good. He started crawling toward me. When he reached me, as more boots continued running around our truck, it was his turn to whisper into my ear.

"We're underneath a fuel truck," he said.

"It'll be daybreak soon. If we want to give these Germans the slip, we'd better do it while it's still dark," I answered.

We crawled back to either end of the injured man and dragged him back out from beneath the truck. We wedged ourselves beneath each of his arms and raised him to his feet – and directly in the sights of a 12-year-old Hitler Youth's rifle barrel.

His left shoulder patch read "Werwolf Projekt" and his arms were trembling as he trained his sights – for what seemed like an eternity – between Olivier, our injured comrade and then me. It was only then that I noticed the stenciled name stitched on the Canadian soldier's coat, it read: "Le Gras".

"Amerikaner," the boy asked.

"Kanadier," we heard a powerful voice boom in reply. It was Michael.

And from the darkness and predawn fog emerged the imposing frame of the blond-haired man fully armed, glaring at the child with his intense pale-blue eyes and standing in a menacing posture.

The child soldier's trembling magnified and, although it was below freezing and he was just in a light jacket, I noticed his sunken cheeks and wide eyes and thought it must have been more out of fear than cold and it looked like it had been a long time since he'd had a proper meal.

"Scheiße," the boy said, and ran into the woods behind him faster than I've ever seen somebody run before.

"Quickly, and quietly, follow that tree-line for 500 metres then drag him across the forest to the other side," Michael told us as he wrapped some bandages around the man's head.

"I thought he was shot in the chest," I said.

"He is, but he's concussed from the fall after the bullet hit him in the chest and he cut the back of his scalp open, which is why he's bleeding so much," Michael replied without looking at either of us, focusing on tying the bandage tightly but not too much.

"Just go where I told you and someone will help you, don't tell anyone about me," Michael added. "Go <u>now</u>, the sun's about to rise and the Germans will be back to take these trucks. This man is your Great Uncle Louis but his platoon calls him Lou. He's going to have nine kids, and they all have important things to do, but this will only be as long as you keep him alive through the next couple of days. Now go!"

So we entered the Palatinate Forest, one of the biggest in Europe, which was dense and dotted with villages that had been abandoned during the Black Plague epidemic between the 13th and 15th Centuries. It was a beautiful and haunting forest. But dragging an unconscious and bleeding Great Uncle Lou up and down the bunter sandstone of the Vosges ridge, however, wasn't as enchanting.

I was completely disoriented and Olivier wasn't certain whether we were moving in the direction Michael described to us. We felt like the young brother in Jakob and Wilhem Grimm's *Story of the Youth Who Went Forth to Learn What Fear Was.*

By mid-morning, we reached a small clearing in the woods where we saw a farmstead with smoke billowing from its chimney and a barn behind it. By then, Lou had lost a lot of blood, his pulse was shallow and his lips were turning blue.

Time was definitely not on Lou's side and we'd wandered the woods too long to risk looking for another house that we thought might closer fit Michael's description so we agreed that Olivier would stay with our Great Uncle while I would approach the farmhouse by crawling along the treeline for as long as I could and then make a dash for the front door.

I dropped to my belly next to the door, raised my left hand into a fist and pounded on the door as hard as I could three times hoping it would sound authoritative enough to get them to open it but if not and they shot through the door, they might miss my arm if I withdrew it fast enough.

Chapter 10

To my relief, a beautiful teenaged girl with braided blonde hair and hazel eyes gently opened the door and peered out of the small opening she'd made to see who was disturbing their peace. She saw my frightened gaze, and returned it with a bright smile with a full row of pearl-white teeth.

"Amerikaner," she asked.

"Kanadier," I answered.

She opened the door wider and quickly ushered me over the threshold.

"Renata, what's going on here," growled a burly bald man with a walrus moustache.

"Papa, this is a Canadian soldier. He needs our help, I think," the pretty young woman replied.

"Sit below the window sill, none of us can afford you to be seen here," the father said, wiping sweat from his forehead with the sleave of his shirt. "My name is Gunther, and you are?"

"My name is Joaquín, and my brother is out there with another Canadian who's wounded and needs medical attention," I said, darting my eyes around the modest kitchen to see if anyone else was there.

"Don't worry, there's no one else here. Neither are there any doctors," Gunther said, eyeing me as suspiciously as I had been inspecting his home.

"But you're a farmer, aren't you? You know how to mend you livestock's injuries don't you," I asked.

"Yes, but you're asking me to put my family at risk. What guarantees do I have the SS or Werwolf fanatics won't come here and kill us for helping you," he said.

I really didn't know what to say to that. He had a point, and if I were him, I'd be saying the same thing. Then, a chill ran up my spine and an image of Michael suddenly appeared in my mind's eye.

"Michael sent us," I said plainly.

Gunther and Renata stepped back in lockstep and exchanged looks.

"Michael, you say," Gunther replied. "Describe him."

I'll be the first to admit that I'm not as verbal as my older brother, but whatever choice of words I made seemed to convince them that we were worth the risk. Moments later I was sprinting across the clearing back to where Olivier and Lou were waiting for me. Almost as quickly, driven by fear and a shot of adrenaline, we ran back with Lou draped over our shoulders to the sanctuary of the farmhouse.

"What's his blood type," Gunther asked.

"It doesn't matter, Papa, my blood type is O+, I can donate for anyone," Renata interrupted.

"Fine. We don't have much time. Let's get him to the barn, now," the patriarch said.

Between the fatigue, hunger and dissipating adrenaline, I just couldn't hold up anymore and found myself drifting to sleep on a bale of hay as the German man and his daughter tended to our grandfather's elder brother.

The following day was a blur, but on occasion we heard German-speaking men talking among themselves as they passed through the farmstead. Somehow, in spite of their presence, Renata managed to make excuses to come to the barn to tend to the animals and she would sneak in left-over lukewarm soup they had made for the German troops in milk maid canisters.

Lou's breathing was shallow and he had developed a fever, but his pulse was growing stronger.

Renata told us he had lost a lot of blood from the cut to his scalp, and they had given him Bayer-Aspirin for the headache from his concussion.

Miraculously, she told us, they discovered that Lou had a pocket watch that had stopped the bullet from piercing his left lung. She warned us that the German soldiers had wanted to come into the barn to slaughter a cow or pig but Gunther had bought us a bit more time asking if any of them wanted fresh cream with their coffee, dispatching Renata with the rest of the soup in her canister.

"The sun will be setting in half an hour," she explained. "You must go back into the forest once it is dark. It's not safe for you, or for us, as long as you are here. We wish there were more we could do. The SS have done unspeakable things, and now they're desperate so there's no measure to the depths of their depravity."

Lou was the first to speak: "You boys have risked enough for me, get out now, and I'll hide in the loft of the barn."

"You can make it, Lou," Olivier said.

"No, I can't yet. It's taking all my strength just to talk and breathe. My ribs are still throbbing," he said, lifting his shirt to expose a large blue-green-and-yellow bruise on the upper left side of his torso.

"I'll bring you some horse blankets," Renata told Lou. "You must leave the windows in the barn open at all times. The townfolk say that the Hitler Youth Werwolf volunteers are slipping open canisters of Zyklon-B under the doors of suspected members of the resistance."

"Zyklon-B? What's that," I asked.

"It's a pesiticide, but we've been hearing awful rumours that the Nazis have used it on anyone they dislike: Jews, Roma, homosexuals, Slavs, communists, prisoners of war, resistance fighters, and priests," Renata. "The active ingredient is hydrogen cyanide, it releases an odourless poisonous gas that interferes with respiration. This is why it's better to risk Lou getting pneumonia than shutting all the windows and being gassed to death."

I couldn't believe people were capable of hating other people to this point, and the look of shock and disbelief must have shown all over my face.

"These Nazis are not German people, they are barbarians who took over my country through lies, bullying and intimidation," Renata said as she bowed her head in shame.

Olivier and I looked at each other, and then Lou, who had fallen deep into sleep again and probably hadn't heard about the systematic extermination of thousands, maybe even millions of people. The decision was now in our hands and we weren't sure what to do.

"These evil men have murdered more than six million human beings in extermination camps," said the powerful voice of Michael from behind us.

Renata was on her knees, crossing herself and trembling in fear.

"In fact, the grandfather of you step-grandmother was killed in a camp called Dachau not far from here because he was labelled a communist who advocated – peacefully – for social justice," Michael said. "This war is unlike most wars. It is truly a just war."

Renata was back on her feet and spoke now:

"I heard the voice of the Lord, saying, Whom shall I send, and who will go for us? Then I said, Here *am* I; send me," the young woman said. "This is what is written in Isaiah chapter 6, verse 8."

Now it was Olivier who spoke up:

"I'm a pretty good shot, at least in the games I play."

He saw the look I gave him, and he nodded back to me to show he understood not to specify that the game he was referring to was computer software created 70 years in the future. Following his train of thought, I added:

"We can hide in the woods and protect Lou and you and your father so you can sleep at night and we can sleep in the day, hiding under leaves or fallen trees. Renata, just ring your cow bells and tell the soldiers you're missing a Hershey cow from your herd and that'll be our signal that they are headed our way. In the morning we'll be to the east of you so the sun will be in their eyes and that's where we'll sleep. In the afternoon, we'll wake up and work our way to the west of you to put the sun in their eyes at dusk."

Olivier stepped closer to Renata, put his hand on her shoulder and said:

"At night, we'll keep watch over you in case those Werwolf kids try to slip any canisters of Zyklon-B under your door or the barn door. If they do, we'll warn you."

Olivier and I lifted Lou up to the loft of the barn and piled bales of hay around him so that he would be sheltered from the draft and from prying eyes. Renata brought up a bottle of water and what remained of the soup, which had now gone cold.

"It's all we can do for him for now. Let's hope and pray the SS move on elsewhere," Renata said as she dabbed the beads of sweat from Lou's warm forehead. "Joaquín, Olivier, you must go now, the SS could come in here at any moment."

One at a time, we slipped out of the barn then into the treeline to the west of the farmstead. Olivier had always been a night owl and I'm an early riser so we agreed it would be best for him to take the first watch and I would take the second.

Even though I knew my older brother was next to me, it was a fitful few hours of sleep that was disturbed by the ear-piercing screeches of a colony of Barbastelle bats out hunting insects for the night. The regular interval of their sweeps through the area did give the impression that nothing bigger than insects were stirring in the woods this moonlit night.

On occasion, I would hear light crunches in the snow but Olivier would lean over and tell me it was just another squirrel making a dash for the other end of the woods.

Then, we were both startled by the sound of large, powerful wings flapping and sharp talons digging into the girth of a tree branch followed by a series of hoots. We looked up and behind us to our left and it was a majestic Eagle-Owl, with its layered plumage of chestnut, grey, brown and white.

"I can't sleep. Who would have thought a forest could be so noisy and busy at night?" I said as I stretched my arms and back.

"I know, but we're both going to need more sleep if we hope to be alert enough to warn Lou and the farmers," Olivier yawned.

"I will watch over all of you," Michael's voice whispered over our shoulders.

We both turned around and saw nothing but the glowing orange irises of the Eage-Owl perched above us.

"I will put you both into a deep sleep so you can rest," the owl spoke in Michael's voice. "You will need all of your energy to carry him back to his unit."

Neither one of us said a word. Sometimes, you simply have to accept even what seems to be impossible and trust that it will all work out. We drifted off into the deepest sleep we'd had in a long time.

...

The warmth of the early morning's sun rays piercing through the dense forest flickered across our faces. Slowly, we brushed the leaves and dusting of snow off of us and worked our way to the east of the farmstead.

We could see a dozen men in tattered field grey uniforms and knee-high black leather boots gathering outside the farm house, adjusting their backpacks – one of them had a large antenna and must have been a portable radio – as well as their rifles. Some were lighting cigarettes and talking, others were lost in their thoughts. Renata came out with what seemed to be food wrapped in newspaper and handed the parcels out to the small band of men, who thanked her and started walking east – in our direction.

Renata reached for the cow bell but the leader of the group stopped her, saying something that likely amounted to instructing her not to make any noise until they'd been gone a long time – or else. She lay the bell back down on the windowsill.

I was eager to warm up and eat something but Olivier grabbed my right arm and pulled me back to his side.

"I thought I'd seen more of them than that," he whispered, as the dozen men marched into the woods about 100 metres to our right. "Let's wait."

The sun had risen above the crowns of the trees and was reflecting off the glacial lake well below the farmstead when we finally saw two snipers climb down from fully grown Black Alder trees where a pair of Hitler Youth Werwolf waited for them with their other equipment. Seemingly satisfied the woods were clear of Allies, they crossed the clearing, heading east. An Eagle-Owl flew high overhead, and we lost sight of it as it soared to the sun.

"I'm so relieved you didn't come out of the woods until now," Renata said breathlessly after running to greet us. "I meant to warn you, but…"

"We know," I said, stopping her. "We saw their commander warn you."

Olivier put his gear down by the front porch and added:

"How's Lou holding up?"

Lou was still hidden behind a pile of hay bales but his fever had risen. He was shivering and his pulse was weak.

Gunther was on the ground floor of the barn, harnessing a pair of Clydesdales to a wood cart.

"He needs medical attention. Better than what we can offer him. Quickly, hide inside the bales of hay and we will bring you to where we think the Canadian soldiers are now," the farmer called out to us from below.

Chapter 11

Lou spent a week in hospital in Belgium and then was shipped out to England for further treatment of pneumonia and pleurisy. Once he was on the mend, he was redeployed under Operation "Eclipse" to northwest Germany where 21 Army Group formed the Canadian Army Occupation Force maintaining its share of Allied control after the Nazis' unconditional surrender in May 1945.

The German civilians were on the brink of mass starvation after being rationed down to 2,000-calories' worth of food a day by the Nazi dictator – just enough for your body to survive. But soon, we discovered far worse.

Europe was dotted with thousands – some estimated as many as 15,000 – transit, prison-of-war, forced-labour and extermination camps. Those who survived to May 1945 no longer looked like human beings, they were skeletons with skin. An adult man needs around 1,700 calories a day to be able to function. These survivors had somehow managed to deny death on less food than that.

While Lou recovered, we forged ahead with his unit – liberating towns and cities and eventually we reached Konzentrationslager (KZ) Dachau, where our Oma's Opa had been sent. It was just 177 kilometres northeast of her home village, the postcard perfect Bavarian village of Lindau, but it might as well have been worlds away. The place was Hell on Earth.

We were too late.

Too late for him, and more than 31,000 other victims of the Nazi regime.

Located just 16 kilometres northwest of Munich, the birthplace of the National Socialist German Workers' Party (NSDAP) or Nazi Party, this horror of horrors was the master logistical work of Nazi SS-Obersturmbannfuhrer Adolf Eichmann.

While Eichmann evaded Allied capture and snuck onto a passenger ship bound for Buenos Aires under a false name after the Red Cross unwittingly issued him a displaced refugee passport when he misrepresented himself, he would eventually face justice. In 1960, Israeli intelligence agents from Mossad captured him in Argentina, brought him to Israel where he was tried, found guilty and sentenced to a hanging death in 1962.

But the summer and fall of 1945 seemed devoid of humanity, justice or any common decency. These were grim, stomach-turning discoveries. They strengthened our conviction that this had indeed been one of those rare "just," as in justice being done, wars. But it didn't erase the images of such unspeakable atrocities human beings could do to other human beings. Olivier and I now fully appreciated the meaning of "Homo homini lupus est": Man is a wolf to his fellow man.

Part Two
Peace & Prosperity

Chapter 12

Lou was granted leave for Christmas 1945 and made his way to Villeneuve-sur-Yonne in the Bourgogne region of France, southeast of Paris and roughly halfway between Orléans and Troyes, where his uncle Alfred Divorne had invited him to spend the holiday with his relatives.

"You're too young to remember this, but there's a famous poem that was written by a Canadian soldier about Flanders," Lou told us while we walked down Rue de Flandres toward the centre of Villeneuve where we would meet Alfred on the banks of the Yonne River.

"It was written by Lieutenant Colonel John McCrae, a Canadian soldier and doctor, after he presided over his friend Alexis Helmer's funeral during the Second Battle of Ypres in May, 1915, during the Great War," Lou said.

"The poem is why Allied countries wear poppies on their lapels every November 11, to remember those who died defending liberal democracies – cultures based on tolerance and debate, not oppression and hate," he added.

The Frenchmen who walked passed us waved and smiled but were all emaciated and sickly looking – their clothes threadbare despite the biting moist cold air. Alfred and his 4-1/2-year-old daughter fit the same description, but were glad to see us. The girl, Louise, was delighted when Lou handed her a Hershey chocolate bar. It would be one of the first vivid memories of what would be a long life, and the first time she ever tasted chocolate.

We walked back to the farmhouse where Alfred's sons were milking the cows and cleaning the barn. It was Christmas Eve and there was more cleaning and preparing to do in the house for Midnight Mass and the meal that would follow.

Françoise remained in bed with a fever and bronchitis that had stricken her again this winter, like every winter since 1941 when the invading Nazi army had requisitioned most of the food from these and so many other farms. Louis, one of their sons, had just been confirmed for surgery on his hernia next month.

The table was sparse, but it would be a happy Christmas. It would taste of freedom.

"I don't have much food to offer you, but I do have a bottle of Burgundy and a bottle of Champagne," Alfred said as he poured us full glasses of the oak-casked red wine.

Lou placed a reassuring hand on his shoulder and said: "We've had larger rations than you, we're grateful for what you can share. In fact, we insist you keep your fine wines for yourselves."

Alfred chuckled and raised his gaze up to mine.

"You're as stubborn as your mother from Melrand, out west in the Morbhian department," he said. "We insist you celebrate our freedom with you. After all, we owe our freedom to you."

Our Great Grandmother was from the Bretagne region of France, which reached deep into "La Manche" or the English Channel, so many of those people spoke Breton, a Celtic language most closely related to Cornish which was the most spoken language in Britain before English came to dominate the British Isles.

They are a fiercely independent people. Melrand was founded in the Sixth Century and after they expelled their Viking occupiers in the 10th Century, through to the dawn of the 16th Century, it was part of the medieval feudal state known as the Duché de Bretagne until the death of Frañsez II of Bretagne in 1488. In fact, they continued to run their own separate Parliament for nearly 300 years until Le Dauphin, the Sun King Louis XIV ordered it closed in 1771. The Parliament of Bretagne deemed the order unlawful and continued to meet until 1790.

I suppose this is why they call Bretons "têtes de cochons", for their stubborn and independent streak.

We had all been living under harsh conditions. The pressure of making do with so little for so long had been a strain as much on our bodies as on our spirits.

When the champagne bottle's cork popped out under the intense pressure contained by the extra-thick glass to disgorge its intoxicating bubbly contents, it truly was the sound of happiness, as sommeliers often say.

Chapter 13

(Photo courtesy of Yolande Le Gras, née Gamache)

It might have been that I drank too much champagne, but when I looked around and saw Joaquín holding his head and I heard a rhythmic and mechanical clattering I suspected we'd just completed another leap in time.

I looked over in the other direction, I saw a tall man in his late 30s with a big mop of hair on the crown of his head that was close cropped on the sides tinkering with what looked like an Onan horizontal twin powered generator we used to power our military radio transmitters.

But this didn't look like Villeneuve-sur-Yonne.

The sky was big, the land was flat and there were fields of wheat and barley stretching out to the horizon, buffeted by a light summer breeze.

And the man working the generator was wearing overalls, not a uniform.

"Where are we," I asked him as I shook the cobwebs from my head.

"You're on my farm," the wiry young man replied, shooting a puzzled glance at us over his shoulder. "You and your brother showed up out of nowhere last night, looking for a place to stay, so we offered you the only space we had in the shed next to our house."

He spoke French with a Canadian accent, so that told me which side of the Atlantic we were on but no specifics on exactly where we were.

"When we saw your uniforms, we knew we owed you a debt of gratitude for the sacrifices you made for our freedom," he said.

"And we wanted to give you a place to rest, even though it's just a shed with bales of hay," an eight-year-old girl with long dark hair said from the entrance to the shed.

"That's my daughter, Yolande. She insisted we make room for you. She said she had a good feeling about you two. I have a feeling she's right, because we're a month away from harvest and I need help with that and other chores around the farm and my garage," the man added. "My name is Victor. Victor Gamache. Welcome to La Broquerie, Manitoba."

We remembered our father telling us that Joaquín's name was inspired by the patron saint of the church in our paternal grandmother's town and realized that we were meeting her, and her father at what was likely the end of the war.

We got up, brushed the hay off our uniforms and followed them into the farm house.

"My father's a great inventor. Our house will be the first in town to have electricity," the girl who would become our grandmother told us excitedly. "Maybe you could help him with his next project: he's going to install pipes from the well we're going to dig so we'll have running water soon too."

We were rounding the corner of the house, past a patch of rhubarb, when a five-year-old boy came running up to us with a comic book in his hands.

"Will you sign my *Canada Jack* comic book? You fought Nazis too, didn't you," he asked, panting.

"We certainly did," replied Joaquín, reaching for a pen in his breast pocket. The comic book looked like it hadn't yet been opened. It was dated 1946.

Inside the farmhouse, a woman was cooking breakfast on a cast-iron stove when we walked in.

"Richard, leave those soldiers alone. Can't you see they're tired. It's a long trip here from Winnipeg," she said, wiping her hands on her apron. "My name is Marie Anne. Thank you for everything you've done for us."

We settled into our chairs at the long table that dominated the main floor of the two-storey farm house and tucked into our bacon and eggs while Victor told his children about the importance of what we'd done.

"There are three kinds of people in life. Some people are the adopted children of God. They're the sheep. A few people rebel against God and harm that first group of people. And then there's the rarest kind of people: the ones who risk their lives – even though it scares them to do it – to protect the first kind of people from the second kind," he said, looking at Joaquín and me.

"I call them heroes," he said, raising his cup of coffee to us.

Just then I felt a shudder up and down my spine, and so Marie Anne.

"Can someone close the windows, I feel a draft in here," she said over her shoulder as she scrubbed the cast-iron pan over a porcelain bowl filled with soapy water.

Both Yolande and Richard chimed in to reassure her they'd closed all the windows and doors.

"My mother used to tell me that getting goose bumps meant a spirit was passing by," she muttered to herself, without breaking from her scrubbing.

It dawned on me then that we might have a visitor, so I excused myself to go to the outhouse. On the way there, my instincts were proven right. Michael was waiting for me around the sun-drenched windowless east side of the farm house – the end that faced the wheat field and dense forest at the far end. Not another soul was within sight, or earshot.

"I know you and Joaquín are in a hurry to get back to your time and place, but your great grandparents really need a few farm hands right now to get them through the harvest," he said.

"It's up to you, but if you really want to be this family's heroes a few weeks in a small town, without telling too much about yourselves, won't change the course of history," Michael added. "I appeared to them during last night's storm, transfigured to look like you, and they offered you food and shelter even though they're poor."

Chapter 14

Richard was telling us how Canada's *War Exchange Conservation Act* of 1940 set off a whole stable of Canadian comic books, inspired by the creation of "Superman" in *Action Comics* first edition in June 1938. That super hero was drawn by Toronto-born Joe Shuster whose Clark Kent character was the kind of reporter he imagined worked at the *Toronto Daily Star*, the newspaper he delivered door-to-door, as a child.

"After the government decided we couldn't afford to import non-essential things like American comics, if we were going to pay for the war, then we had to come up with our own comic books," Richard explained.

"I wish the insides were in colour too, but I mostly like the stories and the way the people are drawn," he went on.

"My sister Yolande likes *Nelvana of the Northern Lights* because she's telepathic and she can zoom along on the Northern Lights at the speed of light, turn invisible, and melt steel," he said. "But my favourite is *Canada Jack* because he's like you two: he fights Nazis."

Joaquín knew I had been up to something when I stepped away from the breakfast table, so he didn't betray his surprise when I spoke up to make an unexpected offer on behalf of both of us.

"Well, Richard, we beat the Nazis so we need to find something else to do," I said to the young boy. "My brother and I are grateful to your parents for taking us in during last night's storm. We'd be happy to do some work around the farm to show you our gratitude."

Marie Anne turned around from her dish washing and gave an approving nod to her husband.

"I can't pay you men in wages, but we could certainly use some help with the harvest. You always have to get it in faster than the hard frost in mid-September, so the next couple of weeks are going to be busy," Victor said.

"Marie Anne's father owns the only hotel in town. I stayed there when I first opened my garage in La Broquerie, and that's how we met. I know he has a few rooms available and the two old brothers next door give us their war ration tickets for sugar and butter so we can feed you with that and what we grow in the garden."

It was Joaquín's turn to speak:

"We can work the horse-drawn ploughs or whatever else you need us to do. It's good to be in a place without any gunfire for a change."

Pushing off from the table with his arms and then leaning back on the two hind legs of his chair, Victor pulled a small cigar from his pocket and struck a match.

"Well, it's settled then. You'll be our farm hands for a few weeks. I have some extra overalls from the garage so you can keep your uniforms clean," he said, puffing on the sweet-smelling tobacco.

"Why don't you go to the hotel, get settled in, wash up, shave, change clothes and come back for lunch and we'll get started on digging us an artesian well? Yolande will take you there," he said, waving to the little girl to come back in the house from the tree swing he'd fashioned for her out of an old tire and rope.

We walked along with our future grandmother from the farmhouse's front yard to the gravel road that stretched out into a straight line to what seemed to be infinity in both directions.

To the right was what looked like to be an escarpment in the distance and to the left a clutch of low-rising building and a grain elevator.

Yolande explained that the escarpment was the edge of what had been Lake Agassiz, a glacial lake the size of the Black Sea that formed in the last Ice Age 10,000 to 30,000 years ago and had covered a vast area of northern North America.

Warming temperatures over millennia had shrunk the lake while incoming sediment filled the receding body of water. Natural drainage, evaporation or other geophysical processes left behind some of the most fertile and productive farm land on Earth in most places, and elsewhere it left wetlands and deserts like Sandilands to the East and the Carberry Desert in Western Manitoba – where Canadian soldiers trained for desert warfare.

The withdrawal of the ice sheet left more than 100,000 lakes dotting concave Manitoba's landscape and, in some places, rich sediments up to 30 to 40 feet deep, and ranging from gravels to silts, with potable water trapped underneath waiting to be released by enterprising drillers – soon to include us.

This rich, black soil was the same as India's Kashmir Valley and the Imphal basin in the Manipur.

"You really know a lot about this," Joaquín said when she was done relating the geophysical history of her birthplace.

"We've been studying this in school," Yolande said, skipping along the gravel road on the way into La Broquerie. "One day, I'll be a school teacher and I'll be teaching this. I'm just practicing with you."

She really didn't need practice, I thought to myself, she was a natural.

It started me thinking about how we'd been navigating this river of time. The Earth, almost imperceptibly to us, continues to transform its surface over thousands of years while human beings were brief visitors, at best for over a half-dozen decades, and other creatures enjoyed a much shorter stay.

How was it that Joaquín and I had become dislodged in the flow of time, and were skipping from moment to moment like flat stones skipping off the surface of a still lake?

Chapter 15

We had some time before noon, so we told Yolande we would take a nap and find our way back to the farmhouse. It was a brief, but deep, sleep and in that world between consciousness and the mysteries that confounded me, I had a revelation about our journey.

I dreamt of all the creatures and people of the world burrowing through time, a dimension like an ever-expanding globe, passing on their skills and knowledge to the next generation, and so on.

But for Joaquín and me, we'd somehow slipped out of the sphere and were dipping in and out of it. Once outside of the sphere, time stood still and the sphere itself was like a wafer-thin disk made up of an infinite number of slices of images, like Richard's comic book pages, that captured the significant and mundane moments of life.

Time was a tangible object on the disk, but was an unstoppable march forward when inside the sphere. The simplicity of this revelation left me dumbstruck, and reassured because whatever would follow this slice of 1946 – whether we move forward or backward on the disk's slide-rule of time – we would find our way back to our place in time to do whatever it is, was, and always will be that we were meant to do with our lives.

Time had moved the sunlight entering my hotel room window to a position where the ray began to touch my face and the warmth woke me from this dream. At the foot of my bed sat Michael, waiting patiently for me to emerge from my thoughts.

"Showing is usually better than telling, wouldn't you agree," he asked.

I nodded – not wanting to break from my dream by uttering any sound.

He smiled, and seemed to understand. Then he stood up.

"You do have a meaning and mission for your life in your place and time, but for now, you have one while you're here too, so we'd better wake up Joaquín and get to work," Michael said, putting his hand on my shoulder.

Chapter 16

"You would not believe the dream I just had," Joaquín told me as he opened his hotel-room door.

"Try us," I said as Michael followed behind me into his room. "Disk?"

His eyes widened and jaw dropped before he nodded his confirmation.

"There are some mysteries that most people aren't meant to understand, and wouldn't understand in this life," Michael said.

"Have either of you ever wondered what the Le Gras family motto 'Vous Perdez Temps' means," he asked?

"The prolific Claudin de Sermisy composed a song by this title in 1536. He sang for France's King François 1er and England's King Henry VIII. He was even mentioned by François Rabelais in the fourth book in his 16th Century social satire *La vie de Gargantua et de Patagruel* (The Life of Gargantua and Patagruel)," he said.

Vous Perdez Temps	**You're Wasting Your Time**
Vous perdez temps de me dire mal d'elle, Gens qui voulez divertir mon entente : Plus la blâmez, plus je la trouve belle. S'ébahist on, si tant je m'en contente?: La fleur de sa jeunesse A votre avis rien n'est-ce? N'est ce rien que ses grâces? Cessez vos grands audaces, Car mon Amour vaincra votre médire : Tel en médict, qui pour soi la désire.	You're wasting your time, talking so evil about her. You people, who want to loosen my bond: The more you blame her, the more I like her. Are you surprised that I'm content with her? The beauty of her youth, Is that nothing? And her gracefulness, does that not count? Stop your impertinent brutalities, For my Love will overcome all your evil talk: Evil you talk, because you desire her yourself.

"Your family motto doesn't mean you are wasting your time," Michael told us. "It means others are wasting their time if they think they can separate us from those we love."

"Love is the substance that binds all our souls. Love is unchanged by time because it's beyond time," he added. "Some people take an entire lifetime figuring that out. Others never do…"

We looked at each other and we were more convinced than ever to stay here, gladly, to help through the harvest and even longer if that's what it would take to care for our family.

We would get back to our place and time when our work was done. Besides, we were starting to enjoy this adventure.

"What will really surprise you is that the composer of that song was born in the area around Paris known as Île-de-France, near St.

Aspais de Melun – where your great grandmother's family, the Savards, trace their roots back," Michael went on.

"There are no coincidences…Nor is it a coincidence that your grandfather's parents founded the town of St. Claude less than 100 miles west of here 40 years ago when they were immigrating from Europe to Australia," he said.

A knock on the door brought Michael's monologue to an abrupt halt as he stood up and behind the door so Yolande wouldn't see him when we opened up.

It was time for us to be present in this place and time.

Chapter 17

The work was hard and the hours were long those three weeks leading up to the beginning of the harvest, but I hadn't felt so good in a long time.

It must have been the crisp, clean country air and hard work: tossing bales of hay, digging the well, and helping install the plumbing to the farmhouse.

It was also satisfying to do something constructive instead of destructive, something tangible...and sometimes ephemeral.

"You see that," Victor said as he peeled an apple with his hunting knife in the noon hour sun on the edge of a malting barley field. "The birds rolling on their backs in the dirt? You know what that means?"

We both shook our heads.

"You can't see it on the horizon yet," he said between bites in his apple. "But it means there's a rain storm coming soon. Birds roll around in the dirt to keep their feathers from sticking together when it rains." he said.

I squinted my eyes to focus better on the vast horizon stretching out before us from the shade of the big maple tree between the creek and farmhouse where the Yolande and Richard would climb onto the makeshift swing during their play time.

After a short while, I could make out a bank of dark clouds rising from the edge of the earth as the wind rustled around us, and the cattle and pigs in the enclosures behind us drew closer together to give each other shelter.

"I guess we'll spend the afternoon running some electrical wire inside the house and hook it up to the generator. At least until the storm passes," Victor said after swallowing the last slice of apple.

***

Over the course of those weeks, we had learned a lot about paying attention to the signs nature gave us. We learned to take what we needed, and nothing more.

We would come out to the farmhouse before the sun would rise about once a week and quietly walk through the wheat fields, the morning dew settling on the kernels as fog rose from the field. It was idyllic.

Then we would follow Victor into the shadowy forest at the other end of the field and learned to tread carefully on the mossy forest floor and try to avoid snapping any twigs under our steps. Even though we were checking his rabbit traps, we didn't want to alert any animals we were there because they would understand this was our trapping ground.

He also pointed out where to spot wild mushrooms and warned us which ones we should not eat, because they were venomous and killed insects who ate them only to have the mushroom grow inside of them until the point of rupture. Nature's own pesticide was close enough to his fields to protect his crops, he would say with a chuckle.

We witnesses the dry mid-summer weeks turn the stalks of barley and wheat to gold by September from green in August. The protein-rich kernels swelled in size as drought stress forced them to draw as much moisture as possible from the plant.

Now the rain was coming and Victor was pleased.

"A little bit more water and we'll get more kernels off each stalk, and better quality because of the long dry spell this summer," he explained. "We'll be harvesting soon, between tonight's full moon and the harvest moon in October."

Victor explained that the full moon on September 11 marked the period of about 130 days since most farmers sowed their wheat and barley fields – the time it takes those cereals to reach full maturity. While you could let them grow a few days more, you ran the risk of being cheated by the 'great white harvester': a killing frost – temperatures well below freezing for at least two hours.

This is why the full moon after the end of summer, September 21, was nicknamed the 'harvest moon'. If you haven't brought in your wheat and barley crops by then, Mother Nature would do the job for you. All your work since April would be wiped out. Some years the killing frosts came as early as the first half of September. This is when time truly became your enemy. No wonder that, in French, harvest time is referred to as a "campaign" waged against the forces of nature.

"There are only a few tractors around La Broquerie and I can't guarantee we'll be able to borrow one from the richer farmers, so we'll probably have to do this by hand," he explained, rubbing his lower back.

***

By the harvest moon, Thursday October 10, 1946, the entire crop was in the bin, there were electric lights installed throughout the farmhouse and there was running well water pumping into the kitchen and main floor bathroom – all in time for Thanksgiving celebrations that weekend.

"That was a spectacular meteor shower last night," Victor said, as he put down that morning's edition of the *Winnipeg Free Press* his father-in-law had given him from the hotel subscription. "It says here that the Earth passed through the tail of the Giacobini-Zinner Comet, which is why the Americans delayed the launch of their V-2 rocket to tonight."

The Americans had seized the Nazis' *Vergeltungswaffe 2* or "Revenge Weapon 2" rockets at the end of the war, along with the scientists and engineers who had pioneered the world's first long-range guided ballistic missles, in a race to dominate space before the Soviet Union.

"One war barely finished and already another one gearing up…" Victor's voice trailed off as he picked the newspaper back up.

"My father gave me some old suits of his and I tailored them to your sizes, Olivier, Joaquín, so you'll have something nice to wear to the parish's harvest supper this Sunday," Marie Anne said as she came down the stairs from her sewing room upstairs, next to the children's bedrooms.

Saint-Joachim Church had been built in 1898 on Rue Principale of La Broquerie, a town founded by Québécois who had moved to southeastern Manitoba because of the rich soil and cheap land. They built their church in the style of 17th Century rural Québec churches.

The interior vault was skilfully painted in sky blue dotted with cherubim flying from cloud to cloud in such vivid detail that parishioners would sometimes daydream they were sitting on an outdoor park bench looking up at the sky instead of sitting in a pew waiting for communion.

Above the altar, in the horse-shoe shaped recess, was painted a scene of Saint Joachim, the father of the Virgin Mary, over the motto *Le Dieu vivant est au milieu de nous* or "The living God is among us".

These parish harvest-time suppers drew people from miles away, all of them contributing something to the feast. It was a time to give thanks for another successful growing season, celebrate and enjoy the moment. Many young women and men would meet for the first time at these gatherings, and often they would start their own families soon after that.

For Joaquín and me it was a bitter-sweet occasion. We knew that our work here was done and that it would be time to go, perhaps as early as this evening's full moon. Everyone in the Gamache farmhouse sensed it too.

"You know, in the third chapter of the Book of Ecclesiastes it says: 'To every thing there is a season, and a time to every purpose under the heaven'," Marie Anne said as she placed the folded and pressed suits into our arms.

"You've done so much for our family these past weeks we'd like to show you our gratitude and the harvest supper is the greatest celebration we can offer between Easter and Christmas," she added. "But we know young men like you have to get on with making a living and we've offered you all we could. Keep these suits, you might be able to find office jobs in the city."

Richard and Yolande were crying and Victor didn't say much but we had gotten to know him well enough to understand he was sad to see us go too, but accepted that we had to do what we were going to do: move on our separate way.

Chapter 18

It was an odd sensation: floating yet being dragged by an invisible and almost imperceptible force. It was when I looked beside me and saw Joaquín's hair standing on end and gently waving back and forth that I realized we were under water.

The water was so pristine it seemed to each of us as though we were hovering in the air, just a metre off the steep incline of a volcano. That is, until we caught sight of sharks rising from the dark depths below us and the eels peering out of empty lava tubes bored out by the molten rock millennia ago.

We lightly inflated our buoyancy compensators from the air in our Scuba tanks and drifted up to the surface at the same pace as the bubbles of carbon monoxide we were exhaling.

"How did you like your drift dive, guys? Was the current too fast? Did you see a lot of interesting things," asked Geert, our Dutch dive master, as he climbed into the Dhoni.

The coconut-palm timber sail boat is ubiquitous in the waters of the Maldives atolls, Geert told us as the captain yanked on the rip cord of the outboard motor.

"It's quite something really," he said over the rumble of the 25-horsepower engine as it plied the open waters of the Indian Ocean on the outer rim of a circular string of islands, called an atoll.

"Most of the Dhonis are built in Alifushi Raa Atoll. The master carpenter can build one in about two months and doesn't go by a plan, so the skill is passed on by word of mouth to apprentices," he went on, surveying the horizon for any sign of gathering storms. "Did you know that the name Maldives is probably a combination of Sanskrit words - *mālā* which means garland and *dvīpa*, the word for island – makes sense, eh?"

The seas were calm and as blue as the sky overhead. Other than the wind in our faces and the soft rumble of the motor, it was as though time had stood still and we were ants bobbing on the surface of an endless blue fluid plain.

Slowly a minuscule, darker form emerged on nothing more than a sliver of the horizon. As we drew nearer it broke off into a collection of distinctly shaped and sized slivers that eventually revealed themselves as North Malé Atoll.

"We'll enter the shallows of the atoll by the channel at Oblu Island," Geert instructed the ship's captain, then, turning to us, he added:

"I want to get inside the shallow waters because the ring of big islands act like a break water on the ocean waves – in monsoon season you never know when a storm will coming rolling in over us toward Sri Lanka and India."

As we navigated southeast after clearing the channel and kept our sights aligned with Hulhule Island, where large airliners were taking off and landing, Geert pointed out his preferred dive sites in this atoll.

One of those dive sites was a cargo vessel that struck a shallow reef and sat broken amidships no more than 60 feet down in crystal clear waters.

"I brought another Canadian out here recently, Gilbert was his name, for a night dive in the middle of plankton season," Geert said, leaning against the mast.

"We did a morning dive on that wreck so everyone would be familiar with the layout, and then that night we came back. You see plankton glow in the dark, so it's a magical experience to turn your flashlight off and they all light up. It's like what I imagine an astronaut feels when they are walking in space," he said.

The night life on the wreck was distinct as well. He said the school of daytime fish were replaced by octopus, crabs, and prawns teaming all over the fractured and rusting hulk. While 60 feet's depth meant divers needed to make fewer decompression stops, it meant a narrower spectrum of colours during the day. But at night, with flashlights, the ship's hull was covered in bright orange and dark red rust and starfish. Startled octopi either shot ink at the divers and propelled themselves to a safe distance or contorted their bodies and changed the colour of their skin to blend in with their surroundings.

The Dhoni tacked southwest and changed course from Hulhule to Kuda Huraa Island.

"There's a Canadian woman who works at the school on Kuda Huraa. She's been in the Maldives teaching children for the last five years. She could tell you more about what goes on above the surface of the water than I could," Geert told us.

"That island may as well be part of Canada, if you ask me. There's a Four Seasons resort that caters to surfers – Canadian hotel. There's a school for the Maldivian workers' kids that was built by the Canadian government and there's a Canadian school principal," he added. "Maybe you know her? Yolande Le Gras is her name."

Either we were becoming cynical or it had become sufficiently clear to us that wherever and whenever we surfaced at a new place in time, we could count on finding a family member to guide us along.

We knew this must be some times in 1997, the last year of her decade-long development work in tropical countries, because Kuda Huraa was her last assignment before returning to Canada. It was hard to guess what time of year it was since we were so close to the Equator, but at this point, Joaquín and I had learned to go with the flow.

When we drew up to the Kuda Huraa peer, we thanked Geert, the captain and the crew and stepped on to shore.

"Do you think she'll remember us from 1946? She was just a third-grade student," Joaquín asked me.

"She was a very smart third-grade student with an impressive memory," I replied. "She'll remember us."

Like clockwork, when faced with puzzling situations, we heard Michael's voice over our shoulders:

"While you shouldn't lie to your grandmother, in her eyes you will not have aged five decades so she will convince herself that you look almost identical to those two soldiers who showed up miraculously at harvest time when her father needed labourers the most," our protector told us.

Chapter 19

We were still rinsing the salt water off our Scuba equipment in the dive club's soft-water tub when we heard a bell ring and a few dozen children yelling, laughing and running in a playground nearby.

The children smiled big, toothy grins as they waved to us and said "Hello" on their way past us as the local workers hugged them and seemed to be taking them home for lunch. They all wore identical white uniforms – the boys had pants and long-sleeved shirts and the girls had long skirts and short-sleeved blouses.

"We all wear the same school uniform, that way no one has a higher or lower social status," said the voice of an adult woman behind us as we looked at each other, a bit puzzled by the children who had just passed us by.

When we turned around, we recognized our grandmother Yolande from photos our father had shown us of her when she worked in the Maldives. The moment of truth had arrived.

"Have we met before," she said, registering a faint sign of recognition on her face.

"Not before today," I said, flashing four fingers at Olivier as he turned around in the hope this would remind him that he wouldn't be born for more than four years from now.

He looked puzzled but seemed to decide to let me do the talking.

"You look so much like two young men who helped my father with the harvest, but that was a long time ago," Yolande's voice trailed off.

"I guess you'd be what we call back home 'dead ringers' – where I grew up sometimes people would try to sell us horses under a false name and pedigree, passing them off for a more expensive one, and the animals were known as 'ringers'. The ones that looked identical were called 'dead ringers'," she explained.

"I'm sorry, I should introduce myself. I'm Yolande Le Gras, principal of the Kuda Huraa School," she said, extended her right hand out to us.

Stammering out my reply to this predictable, but unanticipated, question, I said: "I'm Jack…and this is my brother…Owen."

Judging from the look on his face, I could tell Olivier was going to take some time to warm up to his new name.

"Well, I'm pleased to meet you," Yolande said. "What brings you to Kuda Huraa? Are you on holiday at the resort?"

"We're just passing time here, really," my older brother said, having appeared to figure out that he hadn't been born quite yet.

"It's certainly one of the best places in the world for Scuba diving," she said, nodding to our equipment that was drying above the soft-water tub. "Geert told me there are more than 700 species of fish, and then there's the variety of coral on the reef. I go snorkelling as often as my workload allows me."

I had an idea, and couldn't consult Olivier, so I took the initiative.

"We'd love to keep exploring these waters, but we don't have much money, or a place to stay," I explained.

She put her left hand on her hip and stroked her chin with her right hand.

"I could talk to Mr. Dean, he manages the resort where the parents of my students work, and see if they have a hut to spare. The Canadian government granted me money to build an extension to the school and having a few extra labourers could move things along faster. Would this be of interest to you," she asked.

"Absolutely," Olivier said without hesitation.

"Whatever the brick mason needs us to do, we'd be glad to help so we can stay a little longer on this paradise on Earth," I chimed in.

With a big smile, our future grandmother gave both of us a hug.

"Come, follow me. I'll introduce you to Mr. Dean, then we can talk with Shadu, he's the mason in charge of the project," she said.

Mr. Dean was very pleased with our offer to help as it meant he could keep more resort staff on their regular jobs than on the construction site, and he fortunately had one two-bedroom hut available within the resort compound.

As it turned out, Shadu was the only construction worker on the site who wasn't an employee of the resort. Bricklaying may be an ancient profession but even after centuries it requires specialized training, which meant that Shadu was a man in demand and the sooner he could be done here, he had to tend to other building needs on other islands.

Shadu taught us a few of the basic skills to move the project along like showing us how much water to pour into the hollowed out top of a pile of cement mix, sand and gravel, since he spoke Dhivehi and we didn't.

Dhivehi is the language spoken by Maldivians and written records go back eight centuries, although the symbols used in the script of this Indo-Aryan language can be traced back about 2,000 years.

Masons usually attend a trade school but in Shadu's case we understood from the other workers who spoke English that he had learned as an apprentice to his father, Ahusan.

Over those years at Ahusan's side Shadu learned how to protect homes from the Maldives' high humidity and monsoon rainfalls. Ahusan taught him about thermal insulation and the properties of different construction materials.

We worked with Shadu's apprentice, Pradeep, who showed us how much mortar was enough – and not too much – to bind the cinder blocks we used to build the extension of Yolande's school.

Most days, we worked from 7 O'clock in the morning and took shelter from the blistering sun by 11:30 a.m. for an hour and a half – the time to eat and take a nap in the shade of coconut trees and for the sun to pass from overhead to an angle.

The early afternoons were mostly spent twisting steel wire to bind three long bars of corrugated steel rebar into triangular upright reinforcements that we then place inside the hollows of the cinder blocks before capping off the day's work by pouring fresh cement into that space.

It was a reinforcement technique used all over the world. Our father had described this method to us from the Habitat for Humanity home construction he had done in Sri Lanka and Guatemala.

It felt good to do something tangible, and long-lasting, for the good of a community less fortunate than our own.

Yolande's students would climb the trees at lunch time to find us fresh coconuts – known as *kalpa vriksha* in Sanskrit, meaning "the tree which gives all that is necessary for living". Nearly every part can be used: the water, milk, flesh, sugar and oil. Even the husks and leaves are often used as materials in furniture and decoration. The milk and water were delicious after a long morning working in the sun.

As the extension reached the top of the school house, it marked the drawing down of our time on Kuda Huraa but we only had to look at Yolande to know she realized our departure was at hand.

"Mr. Dean is very grateful to you for helping Shadu and Pradeep," she told us one day on our lunch break. "Tomorrow the walls will be completed, and to show you his gratitude, Mr. Dean has asked Geert to take you on a night dive on a shipwreck."

I began to explain that it wasn't necessary but she stopped me in mid-sentence.

"If he didn't already insist, then I would. You haven't just built an extension to the school. You've built trust and admiration among the islanders. Not many foreigners would do what you have done for them," she said.

So, the matter was settled.

Chapter 20

There was a full moon in the forecast for Saturday, July 19, 1997, along with a cloudless sky which promised a top-lit spectacle beneath the surface.

The Dutch diver jumped into the water first to ensure there were no schools of jellyfish and surfaced to give us the all clear. We descended into the dark depths and turned our underwater flashlights on. About half way down, Geert gave us the time-out hand signal and then motioned for us to turn off our flashlights.

Slowly, the water around us lite up with thousands of tiny specs of light – it was a bloom of bioluminescent phytoplankton. It was as if they were synchronized to a single dimmer switch and it truly felt like we were floating among the constellations. Astronauts have reported that some blooms are so large that the calcium they produce refracts the light of the sun in a way that changes the colour of the water and can be seen from space. And here we were in the middle of it!

We reached the bow of the broken hulk and the bloom started to fade into a fog. That's when it happened again.

I heard footsteps behind me, and realized that I was on the bow of a ship but it was cruising at 13 knots on the open sea.

"Quite a sight, the vastness of the sea and the starry sky at night, isn't it" said the man in a thick wool double-breasted black jacket with brass buttons and frost forming around his beard. His shoulder flash read: 'Allan Line Steamship Company Limited'.

"It certainly is," replied Olivier, dressed in a tweed jacket and matching cap, stamping his feet to keep warm.

"I'm Joseph Dutton, Captain of the *S.S. Sardinian*, and you are," he asked.

"My name is Joaquín Le Gras and this is my brother Olivier," I said.

"Ah, the Le Gras de St-Germain family boarded in Liverpool in March. Philippe reserved a first-class berth amidships. You're planning to immigrate to Australia, I believe, but first you have to cross all of Canada," he said. "Long trip."

"I like coming out here at night too, and not just to watch for icebergs. I feel at peace on the sea," the captain said.

A long silence passed before Captain Dutton resumed.

"I wonder what the 20th Century will bring to us," he said, pulling out a pipe and stuffing tobacco into the bowl. "It will be a remarkable century. People are living longer, science is pushing the boundaries of the known farther every day but I can't help but ask in my prayers whether it will be a great or a terrible century."

It was Olivier's turn to speak: "Perhaps it will be both."

Captain Dutton, nicknamed "Holy Joe" by his crew, smiled as he lit his pipe.

"Perhaps you're right. It's only 1898. Who knows what the world will look like in 1998…Thank you, young men, I must continue my night watch rounds. Good night."

The mist enveloped Olivier and me once again and when it dispersed, a nine-year-old girl stood near us, crying. I crouched down and looked her in the eyes.

"What's wrong? Where are your parents," I asked her softly.

Inhaling in quick succession to fight back her tears, the young girl said: "I don't know. I can't remember. It's such a big ship."

Navigating the River of Time

Joaquín suggested we walk around the vessel to see if anything would jog her memory. The *S.S. Sardinian* was a fair sized ship. She had three masts, ran 400 feet long and 42 feet across with nearly 1,000 berths. We could certainly understand why the little girl was upset – it would be difficult to find her parents even in the middle of the day.

"Tell us about yourself," I asked, hoping to figure out whether she came from a family that could afford one of the 120 first-class berths or was among those in the 850 third-class berths.

"My name is Marie Louise Philippot. My parents and I left Melrand in France a few weeks ago to buy a farm in the middle of Canada, in a town called St. Claude in Manitoba," she said.

Joaquín looked at me. This was our Great Grandmother and it was true what our father had told us, that she had immigrated to Canada on the same passenger ship as our Great Grandfather.

After stopping a member of the crew to explain ourselves, we searched through the passenger manifest – it was dated April 1905. We returned the young girl to anxious, but grateful, parents who had been searching in the warmer lower decks near the engine room.

We were exhausted, and we didn't have a berth, so we fell asleep on benches at the stern of the iron ship, swayed by the gently rolling sea and the hypnotizing pitch of the single screw engine.

It was the sound of children's laughter that woke us but the view from the bench is what roused us to our feet: a grey sandy beach dotted with rugged coastal outcroppings and windswept tree lines. We weren't on the bow of the *S.S. Sardinian* anymore.

"Done with your nap," asked our Oma Ilse.

"Come down to the beach with me and we'll run on the wet sand," our grandfather André said, leading the way past a sign that read 'Cannon Beach, Oregon'.

Our Grandfather had run nine marathons including Berlin, Chicago, Washington DC, New York, and Montreal, so we knew we could be in for a long run with him. He had also walked the 800 kilometre Santiago de Compostela pilgrimage three times, so even suggesting walking on the beach with him meant a serious commitment, but we always enjoyed listening to his stories, so we agreed.

There they were, along with our uncle Marc, aunt Carmie and their children Max, Rebecca and Sophia running along the beach with kites.

"Hey, sleepy heads, did you have good dreams," asked our father, Gilbert, who stood at the side of the bench alongside another man.

"Thanks Michael, you brought my boys back just in time," Gilbert said. "You truly are an Angel."

Epilogue

"Il n'y a que deux puissances dans le monde : le sabre et l'esprit. J'entends par l'esprit les institutions civiles et religieuses. A la longue, le sabre est toujours battu par l'esprit. - There are but two powers in the world, the sword and the spirit. In the long run the sword is always beaten by the spirit."

- Napoleon Bonaparte

Edwards Brothers Malloy
Oxnard, CA USA
July 6, 2015